The LOST and FOUND WEEKEND

BY KIKI THORPE
ILLUSTRATED BY BARBARA BONGINI

Kane Press
New York

For my dad, a great outdoorsman. And for Bobbi Ann, who rocks a needle and thread.—K.T.

To Lorenzo and Caterina, my loves.—B.B.

Library of Congress Cataloging-in-Publication Data
Names: Thorpe, Kiki, author. | Bongini, Barbara, illustrator.
Title: The lost and found weekend / by Kiki Thorpe ; illustrated by Barbara Bongini.
Description: New York : Kane Press, 2019. | Series: Makers make it work |
Summary: Gia and her father's camping trip is nearly ruined by his forgetfulness, but her sewing skills help to save the day.
Identifiers: LCCN 2018023699| ISBN 9781635921168 (pbk) | ISBN 9781635921151 (reinforced library binding) | ISBN 9781635921175 (ebook)
Subjects: | CYAC: Camping—Fiction. | Sewing—Fiction. | Fathers and daughters—Fiction. | Lost and found possessions—Fiction.
Classification: LCC PZ7.T3974 Los 2019 | DDC [E]—dc23
LC record available at https://lccn.loc.gov/2018023699

10 9 8 7 6 5 4 3 2 1

First published in the United States of America in 2019 by Kane Press, Inc.
Printed in China

Book Design: Michelle Martinez

Makers Make It Work is a registered trademark of Kane Press, Inc.

Visit us online at www.kanepress.com

 Like us on Facebook
facebook.com/kanepress

 Follow us on Twitter
@kanepress

"Ready to bag Mount Baldy, Gia?" Dad asked.

"You bet!" I said.

Every summer, Dad and I go camping together. But this year was special. We were going to hike Mount Baldy. It would be the highest mountain I'd ever climbed.

I couldn't wait to go. I even made Dad a special hat for the trip. I sewed the patch on myself with a backstitch.

Sewing is my favorite hobby—next to camping, of course. My sewing kit is super organized. It has a place for everything I need.

There are lots of different kinds of hand stitches, like the running stitch, the backstitch, and the chain stitch.

On the day we left, Grandma came over to say goodbye. "Are you sure you packed everything?" she asked.

Dad is a great outdoorsman, but . . . Well, he's a little absent-minded.

"I don't think there's anything we *didn't* pack," Dad said.

Dad finished loading the car.
I double-checked our list.
We had a tent, fishing rods, and flashlights.
We had backpacks, tackle, and bug spray. We had sleeping bags, sunscreen, and my sewing kit, of course. Only one thing was missing—the key!

Loose button? Torn sleeve?
A sewing kit can be handy
when you're traveling. A
travel kit might include
needles, safety pins, thread,
and a small pair of scissors.

We searched the house. We searched the car. At last I found the key at the bottom of the cooler.

"How did it get in there?" Dad wondered. Grandma and I just shook our heads.

We loaded the car all over again. Finally we were on our way!

By the time we got to our campsite, the sun had gone down.

Uh-oh. Was that thunder?

Just as we got the tent up, the rain started. Suddenly, a gust of wind tore the rain tarp. It flapped loose. Our sleeping bags were going to get soaked!

Good thing I had that sewing kit!

I grabbed a needle and some fishing line and fixed the tear.

"Nice stitching, kiddo," Dad said.

The rain let up by morning, but the sky was still cloudy. Dad didn't want to risk hiking in another storm. We went fishing instead—right after I found Dad's lost tackle box.

Dad's a great fisherman, but I'm still learning. He caught two fish. I caught . . . my shirt. Whoops!

No problem! Back at the campsite, I stitched that shirt up with a whipstitch. It was almost as good as new.

"Next time aim for the fish," Dad joked.

In the morning, we awoke to sunshine. Hooray! It was a great day to climb Mount Baldy.

We loaded our packs. "You have to be ready for anything in the mountains," Dad said.

I looked at my sewing kit. Would I need it on a hike? I tucked a needle and thread in my backpack—just in case.

The first few miles of trail cut through forest. Dad halted suddenly. "Shh. Gia, look," he whispered. Then I saw my first moose!

We stopped for lunch in a beautiful meadow.
"Had enough hiking yet?" Dad asked.
"No way," I told him. "We're going all the
way to the top!"

We looked and looked and looked. But the glasses weren't anywhere. Dad can't drive without them.

"Maybe Grandma can bring me a spare pair," Dad said.

Only guess what else was missing? His phone.

I was starting to think we'd be spending the rest of our lives at Mount Baldy!

Just then the phone rang. It was under the front seat of the car. "How's everything going?" Grandma asked.

I told her about Dad's missing glasses. "Have you checked on top of his head?" she asked.

Bingo!

On the ride home, I thought about our trip.
The lost keys. The lost glasses. The lost cell
phone. It was cool that we made it to the top
of Mount Baldy. But we almost got stranded at
base camp.

I knew I had a new challenge ahead. It wasn't
climbing a bigger mountain—it was helping
Dad!

Dad needed a way to organize his stuff. Something with plenty of pockets. It could have a place for his keys, his glasses, his phone— everything!

I started sketching my ideas as soon as we got home.

I asked Grandma to take me to the thrift store. Why start from scratch when you can upcycle? An old vest was just what I needed!

I had lots of scraps in my ragbag. They would make good pockets. I picked out a sturdy fabric in Dad's favorite color.

Did you outgrow your favorite shirt? Upcycle it! "Upcycling" means reusing old objects to turn them into new, different ones.

Each pocket had to be just the right size.
I made paper patterns to help. The patterns were
a little bigger than the actual pocket would be.
That left room for the seams.

I pinned the patterns on the fabric. Then I cut
around the edges.

A pattern is a guide for
cutting fabric into the
right size and shape.

I'm good at sewing, but I'd never made anything like this before. Grandma was glad to help.

First we hemmed the top of each pocket. I folded each side over a half-inch.

Then I stitched the pocket down.

A hem keeps the edges of fabric from unraveling.

Before adding the pockets, I marked spots for them with a fabric marker. Better safe than sorry!

We used a sewing machine. It's not hard—the key is to go slow! Grandma helped me sew the pockets onto the vest. We put extra stitches at the top corners to make sure the pockets held tight.

For the finishing touch, I added a token from our trip.

"Your father is going to love it," Grandma said.

That night, I gave Dad his present. "It's a life vest," I told him.

"A life vest?" Dad looked confused.

"For everyday life," I explained. I showed him what all the pockets were for.

Dad beamed. "You're a creative kiddo," he told me.

Dad wears his vest all the time now, and not just for hiking trips, either. He wears it to the movies, the grocery store, even the mall!

And you know what? He hasn't lost his keys once.

Too bad we can't say the same thing about the car.

Learn Like a Maker

Gia's camping trip with her dad was full of adventure and almost full of disaster! A tear, a snag, a rip. . . . Luckily, Gia had her sewing kit to fix these problems!

Look Back

- Review pages 8–15. How did Gia use her sewing skills to fix things while she and her dad were on their camping trip?

- Look at Gia's vest design on page 22. What else would you add to the vest to help Gia's dad?

Try This!

Upcycle It

"Upcycling" means reusing old objects by turning them into something different. Gia upcycled an old vest to help her dad keep track of his things. You can make a book bag from an old shirt. You will need an old T-shirt, scissors, thread, and a needle.

Important! Ask a grown-up for permission before cutting the old T-shirt.

- Cut off the sleeves, right inside the seam.
- Cut off the collar, both front and back, making a deep U shape.
- Sew the bottom of the shirt closed. Try using a whipstitch. Or ask a grown-up to help you with a sewing machine.
- Fill your bag with books!